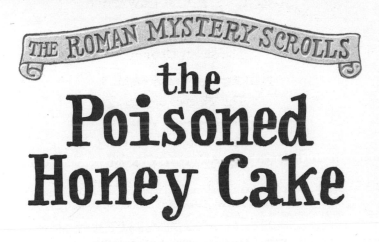

THE ROMAN MYSTERY SCROLLS

the Poisoned Honey Cake

CAROLINE LAWRENCE

Orion
Children's Books

First published in Great Britain in 2012
by Orion Children's Books
a division of the Orion Publishing Group Ltd
Orion House
5 Upper St Martin's Lane
London WC2H 9EA
An Hachette UK company

1 3 5 7 9 10 8 6 4 2

The Orion Publishing Group's policy is to use papers that are natural,
renewable and recyclable products and made from wood grown in
sustainable forests. The logging and manufacturing processes are expected
to conform to the environmental regulations of the country of origin.

A catalogue record for this book
is available from the British Library.

ISBN 978 1 4440 0456 4

Printed in Great Britain by Clays Ltd, St Ives plc

To screenwriter Dom Shaw
and actor Mark Benton
who inspired Floridius the Soothsayer

SCROLL I

THREPTUS THE SOOTHSAYER'S apprentice was hungry.

He was so hungry that his head was dizzy.

He was so hungry that his stomach was groaning.

He was so hungry that he could barely concentrate on the task his mentor had assigned him: to learn a list of bad omens.

It was a cold November morning in the Roman port of Ostia and Threptus was sitting at a small wooden table in a chilly wooden shack. A papyrus scroll and a wax tablet lay open before him. He was supposed to be copying the list from the papyrus onto the tablet. This would help him learn the omens while improving his writing skill.

Ignoring his fiercely rumbling stomach, Threptus gripped the bronze stylus and made a start.

BAD OMEN I – IF LIGHTNING STRIKES YOU

As he copied the letters, he tried to imagine what it would be like to be struck by a bolt from Jupiter. It would be much worse than being hungry, he thought, but at least it would be over quickly. Being hungry seemed to go on and on.

The tip of Threptus's tongue stuck out of his mouth as he carefully etched the words into the thin layer of red-tinted beeswax on the wooden tablet. He was not very good at making his letters neat and small. For this reason, the word 'you' was squished up against the edge of the tablet. A tiny ball of red beeswax had collected on the tip of the bronze stylus. Threptus knew that eating beeswax did not stop hunger, but he was so hungry that he put the pellet in his mouth, anyway, and sucked it.

That stilled his stomach for a moment, but now his teeth had begun to chatter. Putting up the hood of his new cloak – a green woollen paenula – he forced himself to concentrate on the second portent.

BAD OMEN II – IF AN OWL FLIES INDOORS

Threptus looked up at the square hole in the roof above him. His mentor called it a 'compluvium'. It was supposed to let rainwater fall into a shallow pool below. But there was no pool beneath that hole, just the table at which Threptus sat. An owl could easily fly in, if it wanted to. Threptus knew that if this terrible thing happened, you had to catch the owl and nail its wings to the door. He shuddered. He liked owls. He prayed hard that no owl would ever fly into the house.

The next omen required two lines:

BAD OMEN III – IF A VISITOR STEPS OVER YOUR THRESHOLD WITH THE LEFT FOOT

Threptus knew that a 'threshold' was the bottom of a doorway. He had not stepped over many thresholds in his life, for until recently he had been a beggar living from hand to mouth and sleeping in tombs in the graveyard outside the town walls. At least the tombs were dry, thought Threptus, as a gust of damp wind ruffled his hair.

As well as the hole in the roof, there were also several holes in the plank walls of Floridius's shack. His mentor called the high ones 'windows'. He called the one at ground level a 'chicken door'. The only thing coming through the chicken door was a chilly breeze that gusted around Threptus's bare legs.

He turned back to his homework.

BAD OMEN IV – IF SOMEONE SNEEZES ON BOARD SHIP

As Threptus copied the word 'ship', he

4

thought of the big grain ships from Egypt that sailed to nearby Portus. That made him think of bread, and especially of Pistor's famous brown rolls. Pistor added molasses to make them slightly sweet, and sunflower seeds to give them texture. Threptus loved the rolls warm from the ovens and sprinkled with the tangy fish sauce called garum. The thought roused his hunger again, and made his stomach growl so fiercely that he had to press his left hand against it to make it stop.

A fluffy black hen appeared in the chicken door. Her feathery body blocked the hole and stopped the chilly wind coming in.

'Brp, brp!' said the hen. Her long, silky black feathers made it look as if she wore a black fur cape, with a puffy hat and slippers.

'Salve, Aphrodite,' said Threptus with a smile. 'Please come in. It's only bad luck to have an owl in the house, not a hen. But use your right foot.'

'Buuuuurk!' said Aphrodite, coming into the shack. She took small quick steps, but Threptus was almost certain she had followed his instructions.

'Brp, brp?' she said.

'No,' said Threptus. 'Still no food.'

He sighed and began to copy the next omen.

BAD OMEN V – WHEN SACRED CHICKENS
DON'T EAT

'Is it also a bad omen if there's nothing *for* them to eat?' Threptus murmured to himself.

'Buuuurk,' Aphrodite was looking for food under the table. Threptus put down his stylus, picked her up and began to pet her. She submitted quietly and sat like a black puff ball, warm on his lap, her amazing feathers as silky as cat fur.

That reminded Threptus of Felix, the grey kitten who usually curled up in his lap. Felix often went out exploring, but this time he had been gone for three days.

'I wonder if it's a bad omen when your kitten disappears,' he mused. Then he looked down at Aphrodite. 'I don't suppose you've seen Felix?' he said. He knew she loved the kitten, too, and sometimes even warmed him under her wing. She was very maternal.

'Wrrrooow,' said Aphrodite softly.

Threptus's stomach growled loudly.

'I don't suppose you've seen any eggs?' he asked. 'Or laid any?'

'Wrrrooow,' admitted Aphrodite.

Threptus sighed deeply. He and his mentor Floridius had been living on omelettes, but recently all the hens had stopped laying.

'You're not too old to lay, are you?' said Threptus. 'You're the same age as me. Eight isn't old.'

'Brp, brp!' Aphrodite regarded him with a bright black eye beneath her fluffy crown.

'Floridius says hens stop laying after the Ides of November,' murmured Threptus. 'But I think it's because we haven't been feeding you.'

'Brk, brk, brrrk,' agreed Aphrodite quietly.

'Well,' said Threptus, 'that's because we have no food and we have no food because we have no money and we have no money because Floridius gambled it all away on the Greens.'

'Brp, brp?' said Aphrodite.

'The Greens,' explained Threptus, 'are a famous chariot faction up in Rome. Their star charioteer is called Scorpus. He hardly ever loses, but last week his team was fouled and he came last. Floridius put almost all our money on him.'

Aphrodite sat quietly. She was a good listener.

He bent lower and whispered, 'My mother used to gamble, too. And when she lost money, she would beat me.'

'Brrrrrrrrr,' said Aphrodite softly.

'At least Floridius never does that,' said Threptus. 'And he did buy me these almost-new sandals and this nice woollen paenula before he gambled away the money. I suppose I should thank the gods for that.'

'Buuuuurk,' agreed Aphrodite.

Threptus gave the hen an affectionate smile and carefully set her down on the floor of the shack. 'Why don't you have another look and see if you can find something down there?'

Aphrodite clucked softly, and began to search for crumbs she might have overlooked on previous visits.

Outside, a dozen hens began to cackle with excitement. Threptus knew what that meant: his mentor was home.

Sure enough, he heard the familiar voice

saying, 'Hello, me little friends! Hello!'

The hood of Threptus's paenula fell back as he jumped up. He was excited to see his mentor, too. The soothsayer had been summoned early that morning to read the omens for a well-known banker. Floridius had promised to go shopping for dinner on the way home. It would be their first proper meal in two days.

But when Floridius opened the door, Threptus could tell at a glance that something was wrong.

Aulus Probus Floridius was a chubby, cheerful man, but today he looked sadder than Threptus had ever seen him. His straw shopping basket hung limply from his hand and his shoulders slumped. His frayed blue tunic was so pale it looked grey. The stains on his toga seemed even more forlorn than usual and his own paenula was in need of a clean. Saddest of all was his expression. The outer corners of his mouth turned down, the inner ends of his eyebrows turned up and the little frown line between his eyes showed clearly. His face looked like a tragic mask from the theatre.

'Mentor?' said Threptus. 'Has something happened? Are you all right?'

Floridius looked at Threptus and tried to smile, but his bottom lip was quivering and his eyes brimmed with tears.

'No food, no money, and, worst of all, me special powers have gone.'

'**M**E POWERS OF DIVINATION HAVE left me,' said Aulus Probus Floridius.

Threptus frowned for a moment, trying to recall what 'divination' meant. Then he remembered. It meant being able to tell the future.

Floridius slumped heavily onto a wobbly wooden chair. 'I tried to read the omens for a banker today and failed.'

Threptus's heart melted for his master. Floridius was usually so happy.

Recently, Threptus had helped him banish a horrible creature lurking in the sewers of a widow's house. As a reward, the widow had paid them eighty sesterces, a vast fortune! Floridius had bought Threptus an almost-new pair of sandals and the olive-green woollen paenula with its hood and boar's-tooth toggle. For himself he had bought an amphora of mulsum, the spicy, honeyed wine he adored. However, after sampling a few beakers he had gambled away the rest of their money.

Threptus undid the boar's-tooth toggle at the neck of his paenula and pulled it off. The paenula was a big, oval-shaped piece of cloth with a hood sewn on. It was made of thick, waterproof wool and it served as a cloak by day and a blanket by night. Threptus carefully laid the paenula on his bed – he did not want a spark to set it alight – and went to the barrel-shaped clay oven to make his master a hot poculum.

'Do you really have powers of diniv– of vinid– Can you really tell the future?' he asked, as he placed a small pan of water among the glowing coals on the mesh grille on top of the oven.

Floridius nodded. 'I used to be able look at a person and see a fuzzy picture of what they wanted in me head. It was only faint, like a fresco on a wall at dusk, seen from a distance. But it was there.'

Threptus was almost afraid to ask the next question, in case Floridius got angry. Then he remembered that Floridius never got angry, only sad. So he took a deep breath and said, 'If you can see what people want, why do you ask me to spy on them sometimes?'

'If I know a few secrets about a person, it helps me gain their confidence,' said Floridius. 'Remember how useful that information you got on Lucilia proved to be? It got me that permit to practise in the forum.'

Threptus nodded. While hiding in the sewers beneath Ostia's public latrines, he had overheard a magistrate announce his secret desire to marry Lucilia, the beautiful young daughter of Ostia's most important priest. Bato – the magistrate – had been their enemy until Floridius had 'prophesied' that his marriage to Lucilia was the gods' will.

Threptus dipped the knuckle of his right forefinger in the pan to test the water. It was warm, but not yet hot enough to make a poculum.

'It's always good to know people's secrets,' continued Floridius. 'If I tell them something they think nobody else knows, it builds their confidence in me and it helps me get my facts right. Sometimes the fresco in my head seems very fuzzy and far away.'

His shoulders slumped as he absent-mindedly stroked Aphrodite. 'Today, when I tried to prophesy for Liberalis the banker, I had nothing. Not even a fresco at night seen from a mile away. So I made a guess. And I guessed wrong. A little information might have helped this morning.'

'What did you prophesy?' asked Threptus.

Floridius sighed. 'I guessed it was money he was worried about when really it was his little girl. She's almost four years old and hasn't spoken a single word. Not even tata or mama.' Floridius shook his head. 'I started to give the banker some advice. Buy an altar, I said. Put out an offering to a certain god, et cetera, et cetera. But by that time it was too late. He started calling me a fraud and a fake right there in the forum. Couldn't have that, so I made an excuse and came back here.'

'So no food?'

Floridius hung his head. 'No money, no food. Sorry, me little friend. I should have put those fifty sesterces on Castor, not Scorpus.'

Threptus pressed his lips together but said nothing. When the water in the pan was just seething, he tipped some into a clay beaker. He went to a small amphora leaning against the wall. Last week it had been full of mulsum, but now it was almost empty. He poured the last of the spicy, honeyed wine into the beaker of warm water, stirred it with the small wooden spoon, then handed it to Floridius.

Floridius took a sip, and winced. 'Terribly weak,' he said. 'Isn't there any more?'

Threptus shook his head. 'Just dregs.'

Floridius sighed and took another sip. 'Yes, it's important to get the facts on a client first. Can't be a truthsayer if you don't know the facts.'

'Truthsayer? I thought you were a soothsayer.'

'Same thing,' sighed Floridius. 'Truthsayer, soothsayer . . . Oh, what does it matter?' He stared bleakly into his cup.

Threptus took a deep breath and heard himself saying the last thing in the world he wanted to say, 'I could go down into the sewers again and spy on men in the latrine to try to get some more good information.'

Floridius looked up, and his eyes brightened for a moment. Then he shook his head. 'Couldn't ask you to do that, me little friend,' he said. 'It's horrible down there, isn't it?'

Threptus nodded. It *was* horrible down there. It was dark and smelly and full of rats and other things too awful to mention. But he was *so* hungry. His stomach growled again. But weakly. As if it was giving up hope.

'Maybe I could do it one last time,' said Threptus. 'Just so we can get some money for food.'

Floridius looked at him with mournful eyes. 'Poor boy,' he said. 'I was supposed to save you from a life of begging and hardship, but you're worse off than ever. If only I hadn't bet our money on that charioteer!'

Threptus almost nodded. He wondered if he should tell his mentor how foolish it was to gamble. But he knew it would do no good.

Instead he stood up and went to the chair where he had left his olive-green paenula. He stretched out his hand to take it, then drew back. It would be foolish to get his brand new paenula soaking wet in sewer water when it served as his blanket at night, too.

And there was no point wearing his sandals either, they would become sodden and smelly. He sat on the edge of the bed to unlace them.

'Do you want me to come with you?' asked Floridius, draining the last of his hot poculum and getting to his feet.

'No,' said Threptus, standing up. 'I can be sneakier on my own.'

'All right,' said Floridius. He patted Threptus on the head. 'May the gods give you good gossip so that I can earn a few sesterces for our bread. And so that I can help others, as well,' he added. 'The gods won't help us if we only care about ourselves.'

Threptus opened the door – it squeaked on its hinges as usual – and stepped over the threshold, careful to use his right foot even though going out was not as important as coming in.

As soon as he emerged into the yard, a dozen

chickens ran towards him and clucked eagerly.

'Feed us!' they seemed to be saying. 'Feed us!' Even Candida, the white silky hen, came to see what Threptus had. Candida loved to sit on an egg, but today there was not a single egg in the coop.

'I'm sorry,' said Threptus. 'I don't have any food. But I'm going to try to get some good information so that Floridius can be a truthsayer. Then we'll all eat,' he added.

Threptus rolled back the part of the reed fence that served as a gate, then carefully closed it behind him.

As he took a shortcut across a piece of waste ground, mud squelched between the toes of his bare feet. Threptus hardly noticed. He had lived his whole life without shoes and the soles of his feet were almost as tough as leather.

A gust of chilly wind made him shiver and he looked up. It was only an hour or so after noon, but already it seemed to be getting dark. Low, thick clouds covered the sky and there was a smell of rain in the air. Last time he had gone down the sewers it had been a bright, mild day. Today the wind moaned in the eaves of houses and temples, and gusted around the columns of the porticoes.

The Ides of November had come and gone, soon the Saturnalia would be with them. People would be jolly then. But now the cold, overcast weather was depressing. Floridius called these 'donkey days' because they were short and grey. Threptus liked donkeys, but he had seen some sad, overworked ones, and he knew what Floridius meant.

By the time Threptus reached the sewer cover he had already felt the first few drops of rain. Steam rose from the high windows and white domes of the Forum Baths up ahead. He wished he could be there, in the warm steam room, eating a spiced sausage wrapped in a pickled fig leaf. His stomach growled fiercely at the thought, so he gently but firmly punched it, in order to keep it quiet.

Threptus glanced around, but there was nobody by the square sewer cover with its four leaf-shaped holes, and nobody to see him use a thick twig to prise open the cover. It was marble, and heavy, but he finally lifted it from its place. Next he sat on the cold paving stones of the street and used his bare heels to push it away. Then he got onto his hands and knees to look inside. There seemed to be more water in the sewer than last time, and it was running faster. That was bad. But the water looked cleaner.

Threptus told himself that was good.

But still he hesitated.

He did not want to go into the sewer.

In the sky to his left, the unlucky side, Jupiter let go a bolt of lightning. Was it a bad omen? A heartbeat later the king of the gods spoke in his deep rumbling voice. And then the downpour hit Threptus. Within moments he was soaked.

Once again Jupiter threw a bolt, closer this time, and clapped his thunderous hands.

Threptus took a deep breath, made the sign against evil, spat for good luck, and jumped into the sewer.

SCROLL III

AS THREPTUS HIT THE WATER HE gasped from the coldness of it.

Two weeks before, the water hadn't even reached his knees. Now it was almost at hip level. He bent his head so he wouldn't bang it on the vaulted brick roof of the sewer. Then he began to slosh along the dim tunnel in the direction of the forica, the communal toilets.

Without the bright sun shining up above it was much dimmer down here. Almost black.

The dark sewer grew a little brighter as he came to the only part where he could stand upright. Now he was underneath Ostia's most opulent public toilets.

He looked up, expecting to see the bottoms of many men framed by the circular holes on the marble toilet bench above. But there were only three bottoms there and not one of their owners was talking.

Threptus remembered there were other toilets inside the baths. Maybe that was where all the important men were on this cold November day: in the warm latrines by the sudatorium, not these cold latrines that could only be reached from the street.

A steaming gush of scented water from the drain beneath the far end of the latrine must have been hot, because the icy water suddenly became tepid. That water came from the floor of the caldarium, the room where men rinsed themselves with hot water. Now that the water was warmer, the smell made Threptus gag. It was a sickly mixture of myrtle oil, pee and poo.

Threptus tried breathing through his mouth. That helped a little, until someone in the forica was sick.

A stream of yellowish vomit poured down from one of the holes above and spattered Threptus's shoulder. He jumped aside, making the water slosh back and forth, soaking him up to the armpits.

From above, he heard the voices of men cursing and grumbling.

'Do it outside, why don't you?' came one angry voice.

Three sponge-sticks appeared and wiped three bottoms. Then the sponge-sticks retreated, the bottoms rose and the revolving door squeaked on its central hinge.

The only man left in Ostia's public toilet was still being sick.

Naso, Ostia's town bully, had once claimed that a vomitorium was a room where rich Romans went to be sick so they could eat more food. Threptus found out later that Naso had been lying. *Vomitorium* was just a fancy word for the exit at a theatre or arena. But ever since that day, Threptus had never been able to get that image out of his head: a special room for people so rich that they had to vomit up one meal to make room for another.

At the thought, his stomach whimpered.

Threptus forced himself to stay in the smelly water below the toilets. But the squeaking hinge of the revolving door told him that those coming in immediately went out. Threptus guessed the smell was just as bad up there, maybe worse. He pitied Turdus, the slave who cleaned these latrines.

Threptus sighed. Nobody was going to linger in the smelly forica long enough to have an interesting conversation. He had endured the cold filthy water, the stench and the vomit for nothing. He had to admit defeat.

He turned and started back towards the sewer cover. A faint flicker of white light briefly lit the slimy brick walls. More lightning. The muffled sound of thunder told him that up top it had been raining all this time. He was within sight of the place where the sewers divided when he heard another sound: a deep gurgling rumble. And before he could wonder what it was, a wall of water crashed upon him. It swept him off his feet and filled his mouth and nose and eyes. Threptus was upside down, tumbled through a world of icy water, and then his head hit something hard and blackness swallowed him whole.

SCROLL IV

THREPTUS WOKE HIMSELF UP coughing out water. His head throbbed and his lungs burned and the rest of him was soaked and shivering.

'Are you all right, then?' wheezed a voice.

Threptus opened his eyes. He was sitting propped up against a cold marble column in the portico of Claudius near the square sewer cover. The rain was still coming down hard. The storm-slicked street was empty except for a crouching figure in a ragged tunic. It was Turdus, the latrine slave.

'I'm all right,' said Threptus. It hurt his throat to speak. 'What happened?'

'You nearly drowned, then. Didn't nobody ever tell you it's dangerous down there when it rains?' Turdus had a light voice with a kind of whistle in his throat when he spoke. He also had oddly matted hair, bright black eyes and a sharp little nose. But the strangest thing about him was the skin of his face. It was very pale but freckled all over with little brown spots. Not orange freckles, like some people's, but brown ones like the breast of a thrush. It was easy to see why people called him Turdus, after that bird.

'Water goes all gushy during a storm, then,' wheezed Turdus. 'Mustn't go down the tunnels. I saw the sewer cover was open, then. Knew someone was down there.' He gave Threptus a gap-toothed smile. 'I rescued you, then!'

'Thank you,' croaked Threptus. His lungs still hurt from breathing water in and then coughing it out.

Turdus held out his claw-like hand. 'Got a coin for me, then?' he asked, still grinning. 'As a reward, then?'

'Sorry,' said Threptus. 'I don't have anything, not even a quadrans. But if I ever get some money I promise I will find you and reward you.'

'Bah!' snarled Turdus. 'A curse on you if you don't!' He stood up and disappeared into the rain, grumbling to himself as he went.

Threptus swallowed again. It hurt.

Then he stood up and started for home.

He had never felt so miserable. When he was a beggar boy, he had always had a dry tomb to shelter in, or a colonnade. And he had always been able to beg scraps from the food stalls or a coin from a soft-hearted citizen. But now – as a soothsayer's apprentice – he was colder, wetter and smellier than he had ever been. And the hunger had returned, twice as savage as before.

He touched the wax tablet that he always kept down the front of his tunic. It was a gift from his hero, another Ostian beggar boy who had helped people by being a detective. Lupus's wax tablet was Threptus's talisman, his good luck token, his most precious treasure.

'What would Lupus do?' thought Threptus.

Surely Lupus would have tried to look on the bright side.

Threptus tried to look on the bright side.

At least the pelting rain was washing the smell of the sewers from his hair and tunic.

He was almost within sight of the temple of Rome and Augustus, behind which Floridius's shack nestled, when he saw something. A new altar stood beneath a sheltering oak between two rich houses. It was a small portable clay altar of the type you could buy in the potters' quarter. On it lay several objects: a candle, a strangely shaped wedge of clay and a cheesy golden honey cake. The honey cake looked fresh, moist and sweet. Threptus knew the cake was a thanksgiving to one of the gods, because it was on the altar, but also because of the sesame seed letter sprinkled on top. It was G for GRATIAS: Thanks. But to which god?

He looked at the front of the altar and saw that someone had painted a name in neat black letters. Threptus was still learning to read, but he managed to sound out the word: FAB-U-LIN-O. To Fabulinus.

Threptus frowned. He had heard of Jupiter, Apollo and Mercury, but he had never heard of a god by that name. Fabulinus must be a demigod, not a proper god. Threptus pressed his hand against his rumbling stomach, but it didn't help. He was hungrier than he had ever been in his life. And there before him lay a honey cake that nobody would ever eat, dedicated to a god he had never heard of. How much power did a demigod have anyway?

As if in a dream, Threptus reached out his hand and seized the honey cake.

Then he ran.

As soon as he was out of sight around the corner, he stopped and hid behind the column of a portico. He glanced around furtively to make sure nobody was watching, then crammed the honey cake into his mouth. It was dryer than it had looked, and it tasted bitter, not sweet. The smell of it made him sneeze, and when he swallowed, it burned his throat. What a strange-tasting honey cake! But at least it helped to fill the aching hole in his stomach.

Feeling guilty and dejected, and still hungry, Threptus turned for home.

He was within sight of the shack he shared with Floridius, when his feet started behaving strangely. As he started across the small patch of spongy waste ground towards home, his left foot kept tripping his right. He found he was listing to one side, like a rudderless ship. He could see the wooden roofs of the chicken coop, dark and slick with rain, so he headed for that. Aphrodite, Candida and the others would all be huddling there, damp, miserable and hungry. He felt a sudden pang of guilt: he had not saved a single crumb for the hungry hens.

Suddenly his guilt was overwhelmed by a wave of hot dizziness. The world spun around him. He staggered, then fell to his hands and knees on the muddy ground. He panted for a few moments, and then tried to get up, but he felt nauseous and lay down again on his back to let the rain cool his face.

Each drop felt like a tiny cold arrow. He felt sick when he closed his eyes, but it was worse when he opened them. The grey clouds above spun round and round. What was happening to him?

He closed his eyes again and tried to think.

He needed help. He needed his mentor Floridius.

Threptus opened his mouth to cry for help. But only a faint croaking sound emerged. He had no voice.

Another flash of lightning split the sky and Jupiter roared.

The gods were angry.

The gods had turned the stolen honey cake to poison. And then they had struck him mute, just like his idol Lupus.

He was going to die right there in the mud, within sight of his home.

SCROLL V

THREPTUS LAY ON THE MUDDY
ground, waiting for death to carry him
across the River Styx.

The cold darts of rain stung his cheeks and
mingled with his own hot tears.

'Well, well, well,' came a familiar and
unpleasant voice. 'Look what we have here. It's
Threptus the beggar boy.'

Threptus fought a wave of nausea as he opened his eyes.

A face loomed into view. It was an ugly upside-down face, with soaking red hair, spotty skin and a permanent sneer.

Threptus's heart sank. It was Naso, former friend turned bully. Once upon a time, Naso had invited Threptus to join his growing gang of thieves but Threptus had refused. Now there were four of them. Naso, the fourteen-year-old leader. Quintus, his ten-year-old right-hand man. Quartus, the simple-minded, nine-year-old brother of Quintus. And a new boy, with a narrow weasel-like face. He looked about twelve.

'Look, boys,' sneered Naso. 'He's lying in the mud. Why do you think he's doing that?'

Quartus snorted like a pig.

'Good guess, Quartus.' Naso gave a nasty laugh. 'He *is* like a pig, wallowing in the mud.'

'Why don't he get up?' said the weasel-faced boy. 'Why's he just lying there?'

'Because he's a little piggy,' said Naso. 'Squeal, piggy, squeal!'

Quartus gave an enthusiastic imitation of a squealing pig.

'Not you, idiot!' said Naso, giving Quartus a smack on the back of the head. 'Him! I want him to squeal. Go on, Threptus. Squeal!'

Once again, Threptus tried to call Floridius for help, but nothing came. Only a wheezy sigh like air from a deflating bladder-ball.

'Kick him, then, boys!' said Naso. 'Kick him till he squeals.'

The four boys started to kick Threptus as he lay helpless and shivering in the mud.

Until then he had fought off the nausea, but now it could not be ignored. He rose up on one elbow and vomited up the cursed honey cake.

'Urgh!' The weasel-faced boy jumped back. 'He's puked all over my foot!'

Simple-minded Quartus thought this was hilarious and started to crow like a rooster. 'Cock-a-doodle-doo!' he crowed. 'COCK-A-DOODLE-DOO!'

'Shut up, you idiot!' gasped Naso, who was out of breath from kicking. 'Now look what you've done. You've brought his master running. Come on, boys. Let's get out of here.'

Threptus heard their squelchy footsteps retreating. He remained curled up for a moment, allowing the rain to wash away his tears. Then his mentor's face was looming above his.

'Threptus, me little friend!' cried Floridius. 'Are you all right? What have they done to you?'

Threptus tried to tell Floridius he had been poisoned, but his voice had gone. Only breath emerged.

'There, there!' soothed Floridius. 'Don't try to speak. I've got you. I've got you.'

Threptus felt himself being lifted up into Floridius's arms. He felt the comforting warmth of his mentor's plump belly and smelled the familiar odour of sweat, wine and mildew. Now he was being jounced up and down as Floridius hurried back towards the shack.

'By all the gods!' gasped Floridius. 'You're light as garlic paper! Poor boy. I'm a bad, bad mentor, letting you starve away to nothing.'

The jouncing made Threptus nauseous again. He turned his head to vomit, but although his stomach heaved, there was nothing left to throw up. All he could do was retch.

'Poor lad,' wheezed Floridius.

By the time he reached the shack, Floridius was out of breath. He kicked open the part of the fence that acted as a gate, shouldered open the squeaking door of the hut and laid Threptus on the horsehair mattress of his narrow bed. Inside the shack the portable terracotta oven was bravely trying to warm the room, but it was fighting a losing battle against the rain falling through the hole in the roof and the cold wind whistling through the cracks in the plank wall. Threptus felt himself being wrapped in his olive-green paenula, then Floridius added his own faded blue paenula.

Once again Threptus tried to tell his master he had been poisoned, but his voice had fled.

'Don't talk, just rest,' said Floridius. He started to move away but when Threptus plucked desperately at his tunic he bent down. 'What? What is it, me little friend?'

With a great effort, Threptus reached into the neck of his damp tunic and fumbled there. Finally, he pulled out the wax tablet Lupus had given him a few months before. His arms felt as if they were made of lead.

'Oh,' said Floridius. 'Your special tablet! It's all swollen and warped with water.' He gave it a sniff. 'It smells bad, too. Is that what's upset you?'

Threptus shook his head, which made him feel sick again. He took a deep breath and held up his hand for the tablet. Floridius gave it to him. Threptus took it, opened it, plucked the stylus out of the wax and mimed writing something on it.

'Oh, you want a proper wax tablet? One you can write on?' Floridius knew that Lupus's wax tablet was sacrosanct: never to be touched. He fished in his belt pouch and found his own tablet – the one with the grey wax. He opened it and handed it and the stylus to Threptus, who wrote with a trembling hand: POISIN!

'Poison?' cried Floridius. 'You've been poisoned? But how?'

Threptus took a deep breath. His head was throbbing and he felt he wanted to be sick again. He clutched feebly at the wax tablet and used his last morsel of strength to write: HUNY CAK

'A poisoned honey cake? But how? Where? No, don't try to speak. You rest. I'm going to get the doctor. Don't die, Threptus. Don't die or I'll never forgive myself.'

Threptus gave a tiny nod and tried to smile

encouragement at Floridius, but his teeth were chattering too much.

Floridius hurried out, and Threptus closed his eyes.

He did not die.

But he dreamed.

IN HIS DREAM, LUPUS CAME TO HIM. Lupus was ten years old. He had sea-green eyes and dark hair. He looked cheerful.

'Hello, Threptus!' said Lupus.

That was how Threptus knew he was dreaming. In the real world, Lupus had no tongue and couldn't speak.

'Are you carrying on my good work?' Lupus asked.

'I'm trying,' said Threptus, who could also speak in his dream. 'But I got so hungry I stole a honey cake from an altar. I lost my voice.'

Lupus shook his head. 'Stealing is wrong,' he said. 'Stealing from a god is even more wrong.'

'I know,' said Threptus. 'But I was so hungry. I think the honey cake was poisoned and now I'm dying.'

'You're not dying,' said Lupus cheerfully. 'But you'll have to make it up to the god.'

'How?' asked Threptus. 'How can I make it up to the god?'

'You'll have to replace the honey cake you stole,' said Lupus. He looked very solemn as he added, 'And if you want your voice back, you will have to give the god something else. Something very precious to you.'

'What,' said Threptus. 'What can I give him?'

Instead of answering Threptus's question, Lupus said, 'If you ever get hungry again, just eat one of these.' He held up a small papyrus scroll, about the size of a carrot.

Threptus looked at Lupus.

'Go on,' said Lupus. 'Eat it.'

Threptus took the scroll from Lupus's hand and ate it. It was sweet as honey in his mouth, but bitter in his stomach.

'And drink this,' said Lupus, holding out a copper beaker.

'Drink this,' said Lupus again, but his voice was too raspy and he had a strange accent. Threptus felt the clink of a real copper beaker against his teeth. He felt someone lifting up his head so that he could drink.

He took a sip.

It was warm, sweet, spicy wine. Was it mulsum?

'What is it?' came Floridius's voice. 'What are you giving him to drink?'

'Wine sweetened with special honey in which bees have died,' said a Greek-accented man's voice. 'It is the best cure for mad honey. And I added some poppy tears to help him sleep.'

Threptus tried to open his eyes, but they were too heavy. He felt himself being lowered back down onto the bed. The pillow seemed fluffier and the cloak-blankets thicker. He smiled and snuggled down.

Then he slept and slept and slept.

It was the smell of something delicious that pulled him out of sleep. The fragrance filled the whole shack. Threptus's stomach didn't just growl, it roared. He wasn't nauseous any more. He was ravenous.

He could also hear the happy clucking of chickens in the front yard.

Threptus struggled to sit up.

He blinked against the bright light pouring through the compluvium above. It was still cloudy, but at least it wasn't raining. His head felt woolly and his ribs ached where Naso and the boys had kicked him, but the rest of his insides felt calm. He swallowed. It only hurt a little.

'Good morning, sleepy-head!' said Floridius cheerfully. 'It's almost noon. You slept right through the night and well into the next day. How are you feeling today?'

Threptus tried to say 'Better' but nothing came out. So he gave Floridius a weak smile.

Floridius put his hands on his chubby hips and looked down at Threptus with an expression of concern. 'You ate a honey cake dedicated to the demigod Fabulinus, didn't you?'

Threptus was surprised. How did Floridius know that?

'I can be a detective, too,' said Floridius in answer to the look on Threptus's face. 'When you told me you'd eaten a poisoned honey cake, I guessed where it had come from. Remember the banker I was telling you about? The one whose little girl wouldn't speak? I advised him to buy an altar to Fabulinus and make some offerings on it: a candle, a votive tongue and a honey cake. I recommended that he buy one of Pistor's honey cakes. When you wrote the word "poison", I remembered that Pistor makes his sacrificial cakes with "mad honey"!'

Threptus stared wide-eyed at his mentor.

Floridius pulled up the stool and perched by the bed. 'Mad honey,' he said, 'is a special kind of honey from Asia Minor, the province where your friend Lupus now lives. Pistor says a spoonful of this honey makes you dizzy as a spinning top, sick as a dog and weak as a baby. Pistor told me it comes from bees that have fed on oleander. The sneezy smell and bitter taste are supposed to stop people stealing the cakes made with mad honey.'

Threptus hung his head; his hunger had made him devour the cake despite its sneezy smell and bitter taste.

'Some priests eat cakes with mad honey,' continued Floridius, 'because it makes them see visions. But even they have to be very careful. Too much of it can be poisonous. It has been known to kill children.'

Threptus clutched his throat as if to say, 'Will I die?'

Floridius patted Threptus's head. 'Don't worry. You're safe. You were lucky you vomited most of it up.'

Threptus swallowed hard. His greed had almost killed him.

Then a thought occurred to him. By kicking him in the stomach, Naso and his bullies might have saved his life!

His stomach rumbled fiercely.

'Are you hungry?'

Threptus nodded fast and hard.

Floridius grinned. 'How about some chicken soup?'

That's what the delicious smell was – chicken soup! Then the terrible realisation dawned:

Floridius must have killed one of his beloved chickens to make that soup.

'Don't give me those big sad eyes,' tutted Floridius. 'Cleopatra the Second was me oldest hen. She stopped laying long ago. Recently she stopped eating and preening. Hens do that when they know their time has come. I did her a mercy by making it quick and I feel she was happy to do us the favour of giving us this good soup in return.' Floridius went to the pan and raised the wooden spoon to his mouth and took a taste. 'It's wonderful, if I say so meself.' He ladled some into their best unchipped bowl and brought it to Threptus's bedside.

Threptus sat up against the wall behind him and let Floridius feed him the chicken soup.

'You know the saying,' chuckled Floridius. 'When a poor man eats a chicken, one of them must be sick. Ha, ha!' Then his face grew serious as he brought another spoonful to Threptus's mouth. 'Or someone very dear to him.'

It seemed to Threptus that the Cleopatra soup was the most delicious thing he had ever eaten. Better than a hundred honey cakes. Better than a thousand brown rolls sprinkled with garum. It filled him with hope and joy, and warmed him to the tips of his toes.

'Do you like it?' asked Floridius.

Threptus nodded and gave a thumbs-up.

'Good.' Floridius fed Threptus another spoonful. 'It has olive oil, salt, a splash of garum, and best of all, barley. The chickens have had a nice lunch of barley, too.'

Threptus shrugged his shoulders and lifted his palms to the ceiling as if to say, 'How?'

'How could I afford olive oil, fish sauce and barley?' lisped Floridius. 'Ha, ha. I took out a small loan from Rufus and Dexter. But don't you worry about that. You just worry about getting better. The doctor says you got a chill going down the sewers. He asked me how I could allow it. I said I never would again. And I shan't. Do you hear, little friend?' Floridius waggled a plump finger. 'No more going down the sewers.'

Threptus nodded. Then he grasped the bowl of Cleopatra soup in both hands and drank the last bit down. He held the empty bowl out to Floridius and tried to say thank you.

Floridius frowned. 'It's strange but Pistor didn't mention loss of voice as one of the symptoms of mad honey . . .' Then his eyes opened wide. 'Great Juno's beard! Fabulinus is the god of speech. It must have been him what did this to you. You stole his honey cake, so he stole your voice.'

Threptus nodded miserably.

'Oh, dear,' said Floridius. 'He must be very angry with you. But don't you worry,' he added hastily. 'I'll sort it out. In the meantime, have this!' He presented Threptus with a plump golden honey cake.

Threptus took the honey cake. It was heavy with cheese and moist with honey.

'Don't worry,' chuckled Floridius. 'That one's not made with mad honey, just normal honey.'

Threptus sniffed the honey cake. It smelled wonderful! His mouth watered and he opened it to take a bite. Then he paused. He remembered what Lupus had told him in his dream. So he did not devour the honey cake, as he longed to do. Instead, he put it under the paenula he used as a blanket and patted the bump it made.

'Oh? Saving it for later?'

Threptus nodded, and then pretended to yawn.

'Tired?'

Threptus nodded and snuggled under the two cloak-blankets.

'That's right. You sleep,' said Floridius. 'I'm popping out to do a few errands. You just stay there safe in bed. Look! Here's Aphrodite come to keep you company. She's had her lunch, too. Floridius put Aphrodite down on the bed beside Threptus. She happily settled herself over the honey cake bump and closed her eyes and purred.

Threptus closed his eyes, too.

But he opened one just a little when he heard the door hinge squeak.

After Floridius had been gone to the count of one hundred, Threptus carefully lifted Aphrodite off the bump, took out the honey cake and pushed away Floridius's paenula. He still felt weak and his throat still hurt, but he knew what he had to do.

Pulling his own paenula on over his head, he sat on the edge of his low bed to do up his sandals. Then he stood up. For a moment he stood swaying, but the dizziness soon passed. He went to the oven and took a few sips of

Cleopatra soup – tepid from the pan – to give himself strength.

'Buuuuurk?' said Aphrodite, but he ignored her.

Taking a deep breath, he hurried out of the shack. Even though he felt weak and light-headed he was careful to close the reed fence behind him. Then he jogged across the patch of waste ground to the street with the altar to Fabulinus.

In his dream, Lupus had told him what he had to do.

He needed to replace the stolen honey cake.

And he needed to give the angry demigod his most precious possession.

SCROLL VII

THREPTUS STOOD BEFORE THE ALTAR
of Fabulinus and glanced quickly right
and left.

It was afternoon, the hour when Ostians slept
or went to the warm bath-houses, and the street
was deserted. Threptus pulled up the olive-
green hood of his paenula, covering his head as
a mark of respect to the god.

He still felt weak and a little dizzy, and his head throbbed behind his eyes, but he knew he had to do this as soon as possible.

He opened his mouth, hoping that perhaps his voice had returned, but only a raspy wheeze came out. Could the god hear a thought-prayer?

Threptus hoped so.

Dear Fabulinus, he prayed in his mind. *I hope you will forgive me for taking the honey cake from your altar yesterday. Here is one to replace it. One that is not poisoned.*

Threptus carefully placed the golden honey cake on the terracotta altar. He could see now that the clay object there was a model of a tongue. Then he reached into the neck of his tunic and took out his most precious possession. It was the wax tablet Lupus had given him on the day he sailed away from Ostia for good.

Threptus opened it.

Not so long ago, the marks in the yellow beeswax had looked like chicken scratchings. But now that he was learning to read he could see the marks were letters. And they formed words that said:

The letters were slightly smudged and faded, especially where the stylus had stuck to the wax. Threptus took out the bronze stylus and slipped it into his belt pouch.

I'm sorry, Lupus, thought Threptus, blinking back tears. *But you told me to do this in the dream.*

Threptus closed the tablet and placed it reverently on the altar. There was just enough room for it to sit beside the honey cake, candle and clay tongue.

He stared at his precious wax tablet for a moment. Then he turned and started back for home. He felt weak and tired and cold.

But his mood turned from sad to fearful when he heard a familiar voice: 'Ecce! It's that mini-soothsayer, Threptus. And it looks like he's got a fine new cloak!' It was the voice of his enemy, Naso.

Threptus's teeth began to chatter with dread.

'Come on boys! Let's get him!'

Without a moment's hesitation, Threptus turned and ran back up the street, his woollen paenula flapping around him. He darted down the first side street he saw, then up the third narrow passage behind some houses. A blind alley! No escape. But there was a strong old vine climbing up a red brick wall. It continued up past an open window.

Threptus put up the hood of his paenula and clambered up the vine. It was sturdy and hardly creaked under his weight. What was it Floridius had said?

You're as light as garlic paper.

But maybe he was too heavy for the vine, for halfway up he felt the world seem to tip, as if the vine was tearing itself away from the wall. Was it going to fling him down onto the hard paving stones?

No, he was having a dizzy spell. He could also hear a kind of ringing in his ears, like the dying note of a bell, but continuous. He pressed his cheek to the cold, rough brick and gulped air. Presently the world steadied again and the ringing in his ears subsided enough for him to hear running footsteps, at least four pairs of feet. But they ran past and faded away. Praise the gods! They still had not found him.

He climbed as fast as he dared, up and up the vine.

At last he reached the window. It was not barred like many windows in Ostia, probably because it was so small.

Threptus glanced inside. He saw a dim room with a table and chair, and baskets of scrolls on the floor. And it seemed to be deserted.

From the street below came the sound of returning footsteps.

Naso and his gang were coming back!

Threptus prayed a silent prayer, *Please Jupiter, protect me. You too, Fabulinus*, he added. Then he squeezed through the narrow window and tumbled onto the polished wooden floor. He wondered if it was bad luck to enter a room head first.

'Sorry, threshold gods,' he prayed silently, pressing his back against the plaster-covered wall. He wished he had stayed at home, in bed. His heart was pounding like a drum. He felt dizzy and nauseous.

'Told you he didn't go this way,' Naso's harsh voice came floating up from the alley below.

'I'm sure he did.' Threptus recognised the

whiny voice of the weasel-faced boy.

'Well, you were wrong, weren't you?'

'Guess so.'

'Got to listen to the boss, don't you, Mustela, me old son?'

'This way! This way!' cried Quartus, and whinnied like a horse.

Threptus heard their footsteps retreating.

Threptus took a deep, silent breath. And let it out slowly.

As he waited for his heart to stop racing, he looked around the small room. His eyes had adjusted to the dim light and for the first time he noticed that three of the four walls were covered with pigeon-hole type shelves. It was like being inside a giant honeycomb! Each of the holes had at least one scroll sticking out, some had as many as four.

In the wall opposite his little window were wide double-doors. They were firmly shut but the bright thread of light shining through the crack between them hinted at a bright inner courtyard beyond. When those double doors were open, he guessed, the room would be flooded with light.

Threptus noticed that most of the scrolls had leather labels dangling from the ends facing the room. A month ago, the marks on them would have been meaningless, like the chicken scratchings on Lupus's tablet. But now the marks on some of them seemed to leap out at him, as if they were calling him.

One scroll-label in particular caught his eye.

It was not a short name. But it was one he knew well.

GEMINUS, said the label. Threptus knew Marcus Flavius Geminus was the name of a sea-captain in Ostia, the father of Lupus's friend Flavia. Could it be the same person? Then he spotted another tag that read FLORIDIUS – his mentor's name.

Threptus rose cautiously to his feet and took a step forward to look more closely at the scroll-labels. As he slowly sounded out the easiest names, he realised the scrolls were the citizens of Ostia. In alphabetical order! Then he took a step back and looked at the pigeon-holes full of scrolls. There must be hundreds of them. Maybe thousands. Scrolls with information about all the citizens of Ostia.

For a moment, Threptus thought he heard feet on the stairs, but it was only the excited pounding of his heart.

Who was the owner of this house? Or whose private study was this?

Threptus turned to the table and looked for clues. He saw wax tablets, mostly closed and tied and sealed. He counted half a dozen more papyrus scrolls. He noted three inkwells and a silver cup to hold quill pens and a bronze stylus. Beside these were some sticks of sealing wax and a small oil lamp. On one side of the table were blank sheets of papyrus, probably for writing letters. The rest of the table was empty and clean. Threptus had a sudden idea. He looked underneath the table. Sure enough, there was a basket with a crumpled piece of papyrus in it. He took it out and smoothed it down on the wooden floor.

A quick glance showed writing in black ink and beautifully neat, but with some of the words crossed out.

He slowly read the first line, his lips moving as he silently mouthed the words:

P. Lucilius to Bacillus.

Bacillus was a name he knew. It was the name of the lictor who accompanied Bato the magistrate around town. He carried the ceremonial bundle of sticks and axe that showed Bato was important.

But who was P. Lucilius? The name seemed very familiar. Threptus stared up at the beamed ceiling and suddenly he remembered. GAMALA! P. Lucilius was Publius Lucilius Gamala. He was the Priest of Vulcan and also the father of Lucilia, the rich and beautiful girl Bato wanted to marry.

Threptus looked down at the letter again. Most of the words were too big and complicated for him to read quickly. But he saw a few simple words that intrigued him: *baths*, *daughter* and *secret sign*. And one word excited him: the name *Bato*, crossed out.

What to do? Should he stay here and try to decipher it on the spot? What if Gamala came home? Should he take the crumpled letter with him? Gamala might notice it was missing. On the other hand, *it had been thrown away*. To take one of the scrolls would be wrong, but would it be so bad to take something that had been thrown out?

Threptus looked down at the discarded letter. His heart was thumping again and his mouth was dry. This could be the very thing his master needed: a few secrets to give his clients confidence.

Then he heard the sound of voices downstairs. And a dog barking.

Quickly, almost without thinking, he slipped the crumpled sheet of papyrus down the front of his tunic. Then he tiptoed to the window of Gamala's study and eased himself out, feet first.

SCROLL VIII

THREPTUS WAS HALFWAY DOWN THE
vine when he heard footsteps on the side
street below. He froze and pressed himself
against the damp brick wall, hoping that his
olive-green paenula would make him look like
a big grape leaf. Thankfully, the voices passed
beneath him. Slowly – very slowly – Threptus
turned his head and sneaked a look. Nobody.

He eased himself down the rest of the vine.

As he jumped lightly onto the muddy street, the piece of papyrus crinkled.

It was hidden down the front of his tunic where he had once kept Lupus's tablet. Had the god Fabulinus already rewarded him for giving up his precious treasure? No time to consider that now. Naso and his gang might still be on the prowl. Threptus had to get home.

Pulling up the hood of his paenula, he crept to the end of the alley and looked left and right onto the bigger side street. All clear. He emerged, and ran as fast as he could towards the Temple of Rome and Augustus. Floridius had glued hemp rope to the leather soles of his almost-new sandals in order to cover the holes. The repair had an added benefit: it helped Threptus run as silently as the soft rain, which had once again started to fall.

When he arrived back home, he saw Floridius sitting on a stool in the muddy yard, his head in his hands.

'Bk-bk-bk-bk-bk!' said Aphrodite excitedly.

Floridius lifted his head and leapt to his feet. 'Threptus!' he cried. 'Where have you been? I had visions of you wandering in a delirium and falling into the river.'

Threptus shook his head, causing the hood of his paenula to fall back. He hurried inside and excitedly beckoned his mentor to follow.

'Still no voice?' said Floridius. He put the palm of his hand on Threptus's forehead. His plump fingers felt cool. 'You've given yourself a fever! Get back in bed.'

Threptus obediently sat on the bed. Then he fished in the neck of his tunic and brought forth his treasure.

'What's this?' Floridius took the papyrus. As he scanned it, his eyes grew wide. 'Great Juno's beard!' he exclaimed. 'It's the draft of a letter. Gamala wants Bacillus the lictor to spy on his master, Marcus Artorius Bato. Oh, me little friend, this is sent from the gods! Thank you, thank you!' Floridius hugged Threptus. 'Have you read this?'

Threptus wobbled his hand at the wrist, as if to say, 'Only a little.'

Floridius sat on the bed beside him and read it, pointing to each word, even the words that had been crossed out.

P. Lucilius to Bacillus.

I am glad I ~~met~~ saw you in the Baths ~~of Claudius~~ recently. I am ~~delighted~~ pleased that you are willing to help me ~~find out more about Bato~~ with my problem. My daughter is very dear to me and before I consider such an alliance, I need to know ~~some~~ three things my records don't tell me. First, has ~~Bato~~ the magistrate ever acted dishonourably? Second, does he have any bad habits or vices? Third, does he have any outstanding debts?

    Meet me at the first hour past noon on the Kalends of December in the caldarium of the Baths of Claudius. If the answer to any of these questions is YES, give me a secret sign by splashing yourself vigorously with water. If the answer to the first question is YES, splash your head. If the answer to the second is YES, splash your torso. If the answer to the third is YES, splash your feet. If all is well and the answer is NO to all three questions, just sit quietly on a bench. If you splash yourself I will get up and leave ~~and go to a private massage room~~. Follow me, but discreetly. Then you can tell me more. Thank you again for the

offer of your services. You will be ~~handsomely~~
rewarded. VALE.

'Do you know what this means?' Floridius
asked Threptus. 'It means Bacillus has agreed to
inform on Bato for Gamala. And tomorrow is
the Kalends. The day they've arranged to meet
in the Baths of Claudius. This is the opportunity
of a lifetime! What shall I do?'

He stood up and paced back and forth in the
small shack, trying not to tread on any of the
chickens who had wandered inside.

'Eureka!' he cried a moment later. 'I'll go to
the baths and find out if Bacillus answers "yes"
to any of Gamala's questions. If he does, I will
warn Bato. He will surely give me a coin or two
as thanks. I think I can make it work. As for you,
I want you to have another helping of Cleopatra
soup. And stay in bed!'

Threptus nodded, and as he bent over to
untie his sandals, Floridius went to the pot of
steaming soup, lifted off the lid and filled a
bowl. Threptus sat in bed with his back against
the wall and his paenula pulled right up to his
armpits.

He held the warm bowl with both hands and drank from it. The soup was still delicious.

'That's the way,' said Floridius. 'Drink it all. Now drink the last of the doctor's sleeping potion.' He took away the bowl and handed Threptus a copper beaker.

Threptus finished the last inch of dead-honeybee potion and snuggled down into his paenula-blankets. He felt warm and full.

Aphrodite hopped up onto the bed to sit at his feet and warm them.

'I'm going out,' said Floridius. 'Promise you'll stay put this time?'

Threptus nodded happily, and yawned.

Floridius went out.

Threptus snuggled down beneath the two woollen paenulas.

The door squeaked again and Floridius's head reappeared. 'Stay!'

Threptus grinned and nodded.

Having someone who cared about him warmed him more than Cleopatra soup, honeyed wine or even Aphrodite on his feet.

SCROLL IX

THE SQUEAKY HINGE BROUGHT
Threptus out of a deep, long sleep. He
blinked and yawned. He could tell from the
light that it was afternoon again. He must have
slept for nearly a day!

'Sausage, sausage, sausage!' sang Floridius
to the tune of a popular song from a musical
comedy. 'I've brought your favourite spiced

sausages for dinner!'

Threptus sat up and rubbed the sleep from his eyes. He loved spiced sausages. After cheesy honey cakes and garum-sprinkled brown rolls they were his favourite food.

'But first,' said Floridius, 'I must tell you about me triumph!' He sat on the three-legged stool and warmed his hands over the terracotta oven.

'I was very clever! I got to the Baths of Claudius in plenty of time and lurked in a steamy corner with me linen bath sheet over me head. Bacillus the lictor came in first and sat nearby. The traitor! Me disguise was good and he didn't recognise me. Not long after, in comes Gamala – concerned father of the rich and beautiful Lucilia – with a towel around his waist. Not very dignified without his robes. He has knobby knees and a pot-belly, ha ha! As soon as the informer Bacillus saw him, he leapt up and hurried to one of those shell-shaped basins with the cool water and grabbed a scoop and started splashing his tummy. Well, I knew what that meant: it meant Bato had a bad habit or vice Bacillus wanted to tell Gamala about. When Gamala went out and Bacillus followed I knew where they were going, thanks to the draft of the letter you brought me.'

Threptus nodded excitedly. He remembered the letter, too.

'They were going to the private massage room,' said Floridius. 'Well, I know where that is, so I kicked off me bath-clogs and hurried along on me silent bare feet, even though the floor was hot and slippery. Quieter, don't you see?'

Threptus nodded, enthralled by the story.

'It was cooler out of the caldarium,' continued Floridius, 'and there's a bench in the hallway outside the massage-room door, for people to wait their turn on busy days. I sat down there and let me chin sink onto me chest. I snored softly and pretended to be fast asleep in case anyone should come by. There was only a cloth curtain pulled across the door so I could hear everything!'

Threptus beckoned Floridius on.

'It turns out that Bato's only bad habit is that he loves cheese and can't resist it, ha ha! Course, you and I know that if Bato eats cheese it can have unhappy results in the latrine a few hours later, don't we?'

Threptus nodded. He pinched his nose and flapped his right hand, as if at a bad smell. He had once been in the toilets below Bato's bottom and had personally experienced the explosive results of cheese.

Floridius grinned. 'When Bacillus explained what he meant, Gamala roared with laughter. He said if that was the worst fault that could be attached to their "mutual friend" then he had no objections to a "partnership". He said he would call round to see his "future son-in-law" first thing tomorrow. They didn't use any names,' added Floridius, 'in case somebody should walk past or decide to sit on the bench, I suppose.' He gave Threptus a wink.

Threptus grinned.

Floridius put a few pieces of wood in the opening on the side of the small oven and continued his story.

'On me way home from the baths, I dropped by Bato's house on Green Fountain Street.'

Threptus nodded. He knew that Bato had recently bought a house only a few doors down from where Lupus had once lived.

'Shall I tell you what happened?'

Threptus nodded eagerly.

'Well, an old door-slave answered and I told him I had an important message for his master. The old boy shuffled off and pretty soon Bato came out with his napkin in his hand and still chewing a mouthful of food. When he saw it was only me he got all huffy and asked what I meant coming around at dinner time. I said I was just walking by and saw starlings wheeling to the right of his door in a certain significant way, but if he wasn't interested I wouldn't bother him. I turned away, pretending to go, you see?'

Threptus nodded. He could see it all in his head.

'Well, Bato said, "I'm sorry, come in please," and I turned back and said, "No, I can't stop," and he said, "At least tell me what it meant". The birds, that is. I said those wheeling starlings meant he would have an auspicious visitor first thing tomorrow and so he mustn't go out. Well, he snorted and said he is very busy and important and can't loaf about the house all morning waiting for mysterious visitors. I said, "Do as you like, I was just passing on the message". He quickly asked if I could tell him anything more about this so-called visitor and I said that from the way the starlings were grouping I reckoned it was the Priest of Vulcan, his future father-in-law. Well, you can be sure I had his attention now. He pulled out a denarius and thanked me for stopping by and said that if I'm right he'll give me another four tomorrow!'

Floridius ladled out two bowls of soup. 'So I used that denarius to buy some of those spiced sausages you like and your favourite brown rolls and, best of all, more honey cakes!'

'Buuuuurk!' clucked Aphrodite. That must have been chicken language for 'Honey cake crumbs are coming soon!' Threptus heard an excited cackling and then saw a flurry of activity through the chicken door. The chickens in the yard were all trying to squeeze through at once.

Threptus smiled and took a honey cake. He gave it a tentative sniff. It smelled delicious and did not make him sneeze. It tasted delicious, too, all the way down. No bitterness in the back of his throat this time, just the goodness of flour, egg, cheese and non-mad honey.

The sacred chickens had found their way

in and were happily eating the honey-soaked crumbs – a good omen – when Threptus heard a man's voice shouting outside.

'Hello? Does the soothsayer live here? Hello?'

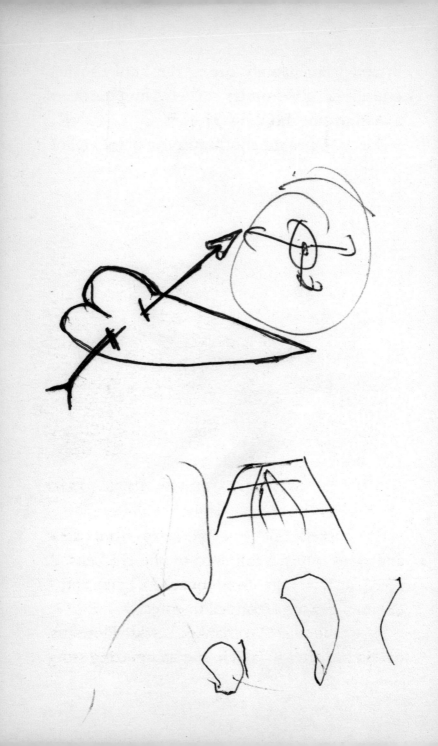

'WHO COULD THAT BE?' SAID Floridius with a frown. 'Wait here.'

He pushed open the squeaky front door and went outside, followed by the chickens. A moment later, the door squeaked again and a tall man in a toga stooped to enter.

'It's Liberalis the banker,' said Floridius, coming in after him. 'He has an amazing story to tell us. I said you would want to hear it.' And to the banker he said, 'Sit. Please, sit.' He pulled up the sturdiest of the two chairs.

'Is this where you live?' said the banker, looking around. Aphrodite and most of the other hens were still searching for stray crumbs.

'It is sufficient for our modest needs,' said Floridius humbly. 'Please tell me apprentice what you told me.'

The banker sat on the chair and, resting his elbows on his knees, he leaned towards Threptus. He had kind eyes.

'I was very rude to your master a few days ago,' he said to Threptus. 'I sought help for my little girl, who is four years old but has never spoken. I confess I thought he was a fraud and said as much.' Liberalis gave a rueful smile. 'But when I got home and told my wife what had happened she said it couldn't hurt to try out the soothsayer's methods. So I bought an altar and dedicated it to Fabulinus, the god of children's speech; a god I'd never heard of before. I dutifully laid out a votive tongue for speech and a candle for illumination and a honey cake for sweetness. The very next day I went out and saw that the god had accepted the honey cake. It had vanished! Yesterday, when I got home from the baths, I saw on the altar a different honey cake and a wax tablet with a message from the god himself. And when I opened the door, my little Marcella looked up from her dinner and spoke to me! For the first time in her entire life, she spoke to me!' Liberalis dabbed his eyes with the hem of his toga. 'My wife burst into tears of joy and I must confess I too wept with happiness.'

Floridius clapped his hands in excitement. 'Tell us what she said! What was her first word?'

Liberalis sat up straight. 'My little girl didn't just say just one word. She said an entire sentence!'

'What?' said Floridius. 'What did she say?'

The banker took a deep breath and paused a moment for dramatic emphasis. 'She said, "Tata, this soup is too hot".' Liberalis looked at them. 'Isn't that wonderful?'

Threptus nodded and gave the banker a thumbs-up.

'And what message did the god leave you on the wax tablet?' asked Floridius, his head tipped to one side.

'It was strange,' said Liberalis. 'There were two commands written on the wax in clear, but almost childlike, letters. The first command was to carry on his good work, and the second to learn to read and write.'

'Oh?' said Floridius, and then, 'Oh!' He turned his wide grey eyes on Threptus, who put a finger to his lips.

Luckily, the banker did not seem to notice their silent exchange of looks. 'Of course, I think that last part of the message is for my daughter. I must make sure she has a good education. I believe she will be a great poetess when she grows up. As for what the god Fabulinus meant when he wrote "CARRY ON MY GOOD WORK", I believe he wants me to use my wealth for the public good.'

'Yes,' said Floridius. 'That always pleases the gods.'

For a moment the banker stared at the floor, then he looked up at Floridius. 'I fear I judged you too harshly the day before last,' he said. 'You were right when you said I had money problems. My problem is that I have too much! The gods have caused me to prosper and it's time I gave something back. Therefore, I am going to build a new public bath-house near the Laurentum Gate, and make it available to all citizens, whether rich or poor. As for you,' he reached in his belt pouch and pulled out a gold coin. 'This is to say thank you for your wise advice.'

Threptus couldn't believe his eyes. The gold coin was an *aureus*, worth one hundred sesterces!

Floridius bowed. 'Thank you, sir,' he said respectfully.

'And here's something for you, too,' said Liberalis to Threptus. He held out a large brass coin.

'Thank you,' croaked Threptus, taking the sestertius.

It took him a moment to realise that his voice had returned.

He looked happily at Floridius, who was giving him a thumbs-up.

His mentor gazed up through the compluvium, lifted his hands to the sky and prayed in a loud voice. 'Praise the demigod Fabulinus, the kind and beneficent giver of voices!'

'Call on me tomorrow at dawn,' said Liberalis to Floridius. 'I would be happy to act as your patron if you don't have one already. I have many friends who could do with your services.'

'Thank you, sir,' said Floridius, with a little bow. 'I would be honoured.'

When the banker had departed, Floridius turned happily to Threptus. 'Do you realise what this means?' he said. 'Me powers might not have departed after all. Liberalis admitted his problem was money, which means me guess was right. Maybe it was inspired. Inspired by the gods!' Floridius did a little dance in the cramped space between his low bed and the terracotta oven, then stopped. 'But I'd better make sure I can still get me prophetic pictures, so I'm going to practise on you.' He fixed Threptus with an intense gaze. 'Hummm. Ummmm. Bummmm,' he intoned quietly, then closed his eyes.

Threptus looked at Floridius with a mixture of excitement and alarm. What would his mentor prophesy for him?

He saw a variety of expressions flit across Floridius's face: a smoothing of the forehead, a frown of puzzlement, a smile and another frown. At last Floridius opened his eyes.

'Did you see any fuzzy frescoes?' Threptus croaked.

'A few in quick succession,' said Floridius. 'Very strange. I saw a thin woman, a honeycomb and a bird. Do you know what any of those might mean?'

Threptus nodded. The thin woman made him think of his mother. The honeycomb made him think of the mad honey he had eaten. But the bird?

'What kind of bird?' asked Threptus. His voice still creaky.

Floridius tipped his head on one side and pursed his lips. Then he said. 'A thrush?'

'Turdus!' cried Threptus, his voice less croaky than before. He held up the sestertius and said, 'I promised to reward him.'

'Then you'd better do so,' said Floridius. 'Put on your new paenula and run to find him and give him what you vowed. By the time you come back,' he added, 'dinner will be ready. Oh, and look!' he cried, pointing to the chicken door. 'Look who's finally back, entering with his right forepaw first, as is right and proper.'

'Felix!' cried Threptus, his voice fully restored. He scooped up the grey kitten and held the warm, purring bundle to his cheek.

Then he looked at his mentor with sparkling eyes. 'I think the gods have stopped being angry with us,' he said.

Floridius nodded happily. 'And the demigods, too!'

*

Threptus in the port of Ostia to Lupus in the port of Ephesus

Greetings! It is me again: Threptus. (You gave me your wax tablet the day you left Ostia.) I have bad news and good news. The bad news is that I dedicated your tablet to the demigod Fabulinus. He is the god of children's first words, in case you didn't know. I stole a honey cake from his altar and he was very angry with me. He punished me by taking away my voice. For a while I knew what it was like not to be able to talk, just like you. When I was ill, you came to me in a dream – yes, you, Lupus! Did you also have a dream that night? You told me to give the god my most precious possession. I took your advice and I gave him the wax tablet that you gave me. (But I kept the stylus.) The good news is this: Fabulinus liked my gift so much that he gave me back my voice and some other blessings, too! So I would like to say thank you for coming to me in my dream, and I am sorry I gave away part of your gift. I am still trying to carry on your good work and I am learning to read and write. I am dictating this letter to my kind mentor Floridius, but I am going to write the final sentence all by myself. I HOPE YOU AND YOUR FRIENDS ARE WELL! VALE.